Last-But-Not-Least

LOLA

GOING GREEN

Last-But-Not-Least

LOLA

GOING GREEN

Christine Pakkala PICTURES BY Paul Hoppe

BOYDS MILLS PRESS

AN IMPRINT OF HIGHLIGHTS

Honesdale, Pennsylvania

Boyds Mills Press
An Imprint of Highlights
815 Church Street
Honesdale, Pennsylvania 18431
Printed in the United States of America
ISBN: 978-1-59078-935-3
Library of Congress Control Number: 2013938848

First edition
The text of this book is set in ITC Novarese Std.
The drawings are done in pen on paper, with digital shading.
10 9 8 7 6 5 4 3 2 1

The text of this book is printed
on recycled materials.

For Cameron
—CP

For Marianna
—PH

CONTENTS

I. SOPPING-WET LAST

MY NAME IS LOLA ZUCKERMAN, AND
Zuckerman means I'm always last. Just like zippers,
zoom, and zebras. Last. Zilch, zeroes, and zombies.

ZZZZZZ when you're too tired to stay awake.
ZZZZZZZ when a bee is about to sting you. Z. Ding-
dong LAST in the alphabet.

That's a problem. I'll tell you why.

My teacher is called Mrs. DeBenedetti. That's
a mouthful so we just call her Mrs. D. And guess
what? She LOVES the alphabet.

Every day Mrs. D. does an A-to-Z roll call. I have to wait and wait and wait. Past the A's, B's, and C's. And the S, T, U, and V's. I have to wait for X, even though NOBODY starts with X. On the first day of school, I told Mrs. D. that my old teacher never had roll call. I told Mrs. D. that it's a big problem for me because I hate waiting.

Mrs. D. says we have to be problem solvers. But how do you solve a problem like Z? I can't just go ahead and switch around the alphabet. I can't start singing *A, B, Z, D, E, F, G.* Somebody would notice.

Today Mom and I are walking all the way to school 'cause we're Going Green. I'm sure I'm not tired. Even though it's three miles. And we've already walked two-and-a-half of them. And I'm huffing fast 'cause a big cloud is getting dark right over my head.

Suddenly I have an idea. I say to Mom, "How 'bout you call me Lola Albertson?"

"No, Lola."

"Lola Adams?"

"No."

"Lola Appleby?"

"No, honey, you're Lola Zuckerman. It's a great last name. Zuckerman means 'sugar man' in German," Mom says.

"It means 'last' in American."

"Isn't last sometimes good? Like when you're last to go to bed? Or last to leave the playground?" Mom asks.

I don't want Mom to feel bad. So I don't tell Mom that going last STINKS, especially at school.

Not all of Mrs. D.'s ideas are stinkers. She told us on Day One that our class was Going Green. That's when you don't make a mess on planet Earth.

Today we're going to write down our three best ideas about Going Green. Then we get to share one . . . just one. Our class is going to vote on the best idea. The winner gets to wear a green vest with a gold medal that says "Captain Green."

And that's not all. The winner gets to have lunch with Mrs. D. in the teacher's lounge. Four years ago my brother, Jack, won the Going Green contest. He said the whole teacher's lounge is one hundred percent candy. And Mrs. D. LOVES candy. When she leans over to check your work, you can smell chocolate right on her breath.

I really, really, really want to win the Going Green contest. I want to be Captain Green. And wear the green vest with the gold medal, just like Jack. I want to have lunch all by myself with Mrs. D., won on won, like she told us. Right inside that teacher's

lounge, full of candy bars and sour fruit tarts and watermelon taffy and chocolate-marshmallow-peanut-butter fudge balls. I want to be the best 'cause that would teach SOMEBODY I know a lesson.

When you're "Z" and your teacher LOVES the alphabet, that's a problem. From A to Z, someone is sure to take all my Going Green ideas.

"Come on, sweetie," Mom says. "You don't want to be late." Mom looks up at the sky, so I do, too. That big cloud is getting darker. "And it looks like rain."

We start walking faster. My legs feel like scissors. *Swish, swish, swishety-swish.*

"Mom, are you sure we're going to get there on time?" I ask. Mom says,

"time gets away from her." She also says, "time flies,"
and, "I don't know where the time went." That's
called "late."

"Sure, I'm sure."

"Real time or Mom time?"
I ask.

Mom looks at her watch. "Let's jog," Mom says.

We start jogging. Now my legs feel like hammers.
Thud, thud, thudety, thud.

Splat. A raindrop falls. Then another. Then another.
Pretty soon it's raining hard.

Not only am I going to be last. I'm going to be
sopping-wet last.

A giant SUV zooms by.

"That's the Andersons' car!" Mom says. "Quick,
Lola, wave your arms!"

I wave my arms and yell, "Stop! Wait! We need a ride."

Penny Anderson used to be our neighbor. Amanda Anderson used to be my best friend. Not anymore.

And it's not because Amanda always gets to go first, in case you think that.

Mom waves her arms. "Wait!"

But Mrs. Anderson's SUV keeps zooming by.

"Oh shoot, she didn't see us," Mom says.

Splat, splat, splat, and a jump over a soggy patch of grass, and Mom has to stop to pick up somebody's water bottle.

Finally, we get to my school. *BRRRRIIIING!*

I am late, late, late. Mrs. Crowley, the secretary, gives me a late pass.

"Late again, Lola," she says.

Late-Again-Lola? "That's not my name," I say, but real quiet. I only missed the bus ONCE last week, 'cause I couldn't find my purple notebook.

I take off doing my special run-skip down the hall. It's handy for getting somewhere fast.

I race in and put my late pass in Mrs. D's basket. Then I zip on over to my desk.

"John Carmine Tabanelli," Mrs. D. says.

"Here," John says. Mrs. D. learned on Day One NOT to skip any parts of John Carmine Tabanelli's name. It's special to him.

"Timo Toivonen."

"I am here," Timo says.

"Ben Wexler."

"Here, " Ben says.

"Lola Zuckerman."

I slip-slide into my seat. "HERE!" I holler.

That's the only good thing about "Z."

In roll call, Mrs. D. gets to me last. So even with a late pass, I still get to yell "HERE!"

Poor ol' Amanda Anderson, Mrs. D. always calls her name first. She better not be late ever!

2. WHAT'S YOUR PROBLEM?

"YOU'RE _SOAKING WET_," HARVEY

Baxter says. Harvey Baxter always tells you stuff you already know, and in a really loud voice. Harvey acts loud, too. He crashes and stomps and thumps.

I shake my head like my dog, Patches. "So what? I walked to school and saved Mother Earth."

"We zoomed right by you on the bus. That was a dumb idea, walking to school."

"No, sir, it wasn't. We were Going Green," I tell him. Then I look over to see if Mrs. D. heard me.

"That's why I'd make the best Captain Green. I'm always thinking green things."

"It's not Captain Green, Lola," Harvey says. "It's green captain. And I'm going to win! I have a great idea."

"Wrong again, Harvey," I say.

"Harvey, Lola, let's put on our listening ears.

What do you hear?" Mrs. D. asks.

"Your voice, telling us to be quiet," Harvey says.

"Anything else?" she asks.

"I hear rain," I say.

"Yes. The pitter-patter of rain," Mrs. D. says.

"I hate rain," Harvey says.

"What's good about rain?" Mrs. D. asks.

"It makes the grass grow," Amanda says.

"And pretty flowers," Jessie says.

"And big, big trees," I say, "lots of trees."

"When a tree catches on fire, you have to get a fire truck to put it out," Ben Wexler says. He shows us how a fire hose works.

"True," Mrs. D. says. "What are some things that grow in September?"

"Apples!" everyone yells. We talked about that last week when we made an A-to-Z fruits-and-vegetables list.

I look over at Amanda Anderson. She has a big smile on her face. Fishsticks! She's happy that her fruit goes first. I decide that I like mangoes a whole lot better than apples.

"It also brings my birthday!" Sam yells out.

"Hand, Sam!" Mrs. D. says.

If you were an alien you would think Mrs. D. is saying "handsome." She isn't.

"Jellybeans, what contest does September bring?" she asks. She has about four hundred nicknames for us.

Mostly candy names. Like I said, she LOVES candy.

"The Going Green contest!" we yell.

Maybe she forgot she told us that yesterday. "That's right," she says, but we are all talking at once. Mrs. D. claps her hands to get everyone's attention: *clap, clap, clap-clap-clap.*

"And how are we going to begin our Going Green contest?" she asks. "Hands, please."

"*OOH OOH OOH*," Sam grunts. His hand is waving back and forth.

Mrs. D. calls on Charlie Henderson.

"We're going to write down three ways we can Go Green," he says. "Then we're going to share one."

Harvey Baxter raises his hand. "Just one?" he asks.

  "Just one, Harvey, but with each of you sharing one, that will be nineteen Going Green ideas."

My stomach starts to ache a tiny bit. Maybe Mrs. D. will go backward today. Maybe "Z" will go first. But I don't get my hopes up. She's got all the fruits and vegetables right up there on her bulletin board from A to Z: apples, bananas, cherries, dates. She's got a whole lot of books lined up in alphabetical order: Adams, Barker, Carver, Dawson. Oh, and guess what? We did self-portraits and she hung them up A to Z. My ear's squished in the corner, and part of my eyeball.

Everywhere you look in Mrs. D's room, the

alphabet stares right back at you.

I get out my new, watermelon-smelling pencil. I had it tucked in the special pencil pocket of my Lola dress. Mom made it—the dress and the pocket—just for me. That's why I always know where my watermelon pencil is. I also have a pocket for notes, and a zipper pocket for my lucky white marble that looks like a dead man's eyeball.

I write, write, write. All around me the air smells like watermelons. I've decided to write down a whole bunch of ideas. I look over at Amanda Anderson and she's already done, 'cause one idea would be okay for Amanda Anderson. One or two or three ideas would be okay for "A" through "Y," but not for "Z." I write:

1. No trash lunch. (And that means no plastic sandwich baggies! No juice boxes. I got that out of *Highlights* magazine. Is that cheating?)

2. Don't flush the toilet. (Unless you go number two—then you better flush it, and I'm talking to you, Jack.) My brother is in sixth grade so he should know better.

3. Shut the door when you come inside! (We're not heating the outdoors, you know!)

4. Shut off the lights when you leave the room! (Don't worry cause Patches can see in the dark.)

5. Make cows stop farting. They gas up the air.

● ● ●

Then Mrs. D. says, "Jujubes, I look forward to hearing all your Going Green problems and your solutions after recess. Now it's time to move on to math."

We move on to math. Then we move on to Spanish, Snack, and Birthday Share. If it's your birthday month you get to share. John Carmine

Tabanelli shares his electric train. We set up the tracks around Mrs. D.'s desk and we watch it go around seventeen times. Then it's recess!

We line up A to Z. I run out there as fast as I can. Too late! Amanda Anderson is already swinging with Jessie Chavez. Amanda's dress is pink with purple polka dots. Jessie's is purple with pink polka dots. Too bad they don't have pockets like mine.

After about four hundred hours, Amanda and Jessie finally wear out. I scooch onto the swing. Amanda is walking away. She's holding hands with Jessie Chavez.

"Um . . . Amanda." I peep that out. Even I can't hear me.

"Want to swing Double Dippers?" I say louder to Amanda. That's where you swing at exactly the same time. We invented that. Maybe.

Amanda stops and turns around. "No thanks," she says. She and Jessie kneel down to make chalk drawings on the wet pavement.

"You drove past and didn't pick us up!" I shout over to Amanda on the down swing.

Amanda draws a tail. "No, sir, I didn't. I don't even know how to drive."

"I mean your mom."

"She didn't see you!"

"I like your dog picture!" I yell.

Amanda gets a mean look on her face. "It's a horse and you know it."

When I was little, I used to swing Double Dippers with Amanda. Now I'm in second grade. Now me and Amanda are like:

1. Mustard and pancakes.
2. Syrup and hot dogs.
3. Broccoli and cotton candy.

We don't go together anymore.

It's all Amanda Anderson's fault. Maybe.

3. OUT OF IDEAS

FINALLY IT'S TIME FOR OUR GOING
Green ideas. I pull out my list that I wrote in my
big purple notebook. *Mmmm.* It still smells like
watermelons.

We get to act like Mrs. D. We get to talk without
raising our hands, and call on people. Amanda
stands at the front of the class in her pink dress
with purple polka dots, and no chalk dust or holes.
Holes just pop right out on my clothes.

"My problem is trash. My solution," Amanda

takes a breath, "is to have a no-trash lunch!"

I cross that one off my list. Fishsticks! Amanda has a subscription to *Highlights*, too. That cheater just stole that idea right out of there. Maybe.

Olivia O'Donnell raises her hand.

"Yes, Olivia?" Amanda says.

"What about juice boxes? Mom packs me Tubby's Juicy Juicers every day."

"Have your Mom buy a big jug of juice and put some in a thermos," Amanda says.

A bunch of people raise their hands, me too. But mean ol' Amanda Anderson doesn't call on me. Too bad, 'cause I want to say that I have that idea in my purple notebook.

Amanda curtsies. She waves to everybody. I pretend to be invisible.

Next, Harvey Baxter hooks his thumbs in his belt loops and leans way back.

"Perfume is bad," he says. "It stinks up all the good air."

"You should shut the door when you come inside," Dilly Chang says. Her real name is Katherine. But when she was little, she loved dill pickles. So now her name is Dilly.

I cross that one off my list. I still have three really good ideas.

Jessie Chavez stands up in her purple dress with pink polka dots.

"I have a great Going Green problem and a really super solution!" Her Mom is in advertising and Jessie always talks like a TV commercial.

"Let's hear it," Mrs. D. says in her plain biscuit voice.

"Pool heaters!"

Mrs. D. asks, "Pool heaters?"

"Sure! Can't you swim in your pool without the heat on? Well, I can! So turn off your pool heater and save energy!" Jessie Chavez gives a big smile.

I raise my hand and holler, "I don't have a pool, so how can I turn off my pool heater?"

"Me neither!" a whole bunch of people yell.

Jessie's mouth gets crumpled like a used tissue.

Amanda Anderson raises her hand and yells, "I do! And I think it's a great idea, Jessie!"

"Well I don't," I say on the loud side.

"Thank you, Jessie," Mrs. D. says. She gives me THE LOOK.

Next, Abby Frank stands by the door, chewing on her braid. She's a chewer, that Abby Frank. She chews the erasers right off pencils.

"People waste energy by leaving on the lights." She reaches for the light switch. *Flip!*

"Abby," Mrs. D. says, "we can't see."

Abby turns on the lights. Now she's got both of

her braids stuffed in her mouth.

Charlie Henderson asks, "Did you know if you flush the toilet every time you pee you waste five gallons of water? I read that on the Internet." He loves facts from the Internet.

"And if you don't, *PEE YOO*," Harvey calls out.

I cross that one off my list. All I've got left is cow gas.

Sam Noonan says playing video games uses a lot of energy. "Go outside and ride your bike," he says.

"My baby brother uses lots of diapers," Sophie Nunez says. She plugs her nose. "I'm going to ask my mom to use cloth diapers."

Olivia O'Donnell says taking long showers is bad. It wastes water.

"We probably shouldn't take showers or baths period," Sam says.

Cow gas, cow gas, please, nobody take cow gas.

Madison Rogers reads hers. "Timo told me at recess that people in Finland don't have big jars of peanut butter. I am very sad that people in Finland don't have big jars of peanut butter. They only have teeny-weeny ones. They can't get full without gobs of peanut butter. They have to eat nothing-and-J sandwiches."

"I love peanut butter!" Harvey Baxter calls.

Ruby Snow yells, "I hate peanut butter! I want to move to Finland!"

"Peanut butter! Peanut butter!" we peanut-butter people chant.

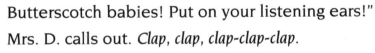

"Yuck! Yuck! Yuck!" Ruby, Charlie, and Sam yell.

"Butterscotch babies! Butterscotch babies! Put on your listening ears!" Mrs. D. calls out. *Clap, clap, clap-clap-clap.*

We stop peanut-butter talking and clap along with Mrs. D. She takes a deep breath. "Madison, thank you for caring, but that really isn't a Going Green problem. Do you have another Going Green idea?"

Madison groans. "All my good ideas got taken up, 'cause I'm 'R' for Rogers."

Fishsticks! She thinks she has problems! Try being "Z."

Madison says, "Hmmmm. I have one more, but it might not be a good one. How about cow flatulence? My dad said cow flatulence pollutes the air."

I raise my hand. Madison calls on me.

"Is flatulence the same thing as a fart?"

Madison thinks for a minute. "Um, I don't think so." She looks at Mrs. D.

"Yes, it is," Mrs. D. says really fast.

OH NO. I cross it off my list.

"Good one," Mrs. D. calls over all the armpit farting going on in the room.

"Who's next?"

I know.

Rita Rohan. She says we should ride horses to school, but she'd have to give everyone a ride 'cause she's the only one who has a horse.

Now it's time for the "S" people. That's Ari Shapiro, Ruby Snow, Gwendolyn Swanson-Carmichael, and Jamal Stevenson. That Jamal is gifted-n-talented. We took a test and it said so.

Then John Carmine Tabanelli and Timo Toivonen and Ben Wexler have their turns.

After that, it's me.

I'm last.

Zuckerman. Zuckerman. Zuckerman.

The worst name in the world.

I will always be last, and out of ideas. That's when I hear ol' Amanda Anderson all the way across the room. "It's easy to pack a trash-free lunch!"

"You already had your turn, Amanda Anderson!" I yell.

Fishsticks!

I want to beat Amanda Anderson. Not with a stick, in case you think that. I want to win. And I want her to lose. I want to beat, beat, beat her. And only I know why I want to beat Amanda Anderson.

3½. WHY I WANT TO BEAT AMANDA ANDERSON

I KNOW AMANDA ANDERSON.

I know all the things Amanda loves, even:

1. Smelly lotion. (*Blech*!)
2. Bows and ribbons. (Who needs 'em?)
3. Princess stories. (No thanks!)
4. Brownly bananas. (Yellow, thank you.)

Yes, I know EVERYTHING about Amanda Anderson. I used to be Amanda's next door neighbor AND her best friend. I spent the night at Amanda Anderson's house forty-four and one-half times. The one-half was because of the night we ate chicken teriyaki and I threw it up. I had to go home. The other forty-four times worked out great.

She had a house with three bedrooms and two bathrooms; same as us, but with different wallpaper. Even when me and Amanda were babies, we were best friends. We had a secret Peanut Butter and Jelly handshake. We said, "Ooga booga! Ooga! Booga!" when we wanted to get wild.

Then the Andersons moved! They moved to a house on Windy Hill Drive with six bathrooms. We stayed in our good ol' house on Cherry Tree Lane. We've got one extra room for grandparents and Mom's sewing machine, and nothing else extra. We're squeezed in like sardines, but Dad says we like to be cozy. Now we just have a sewing machine in that extra room, 'cause Granny and Grampy went home.

I went over for a play date at the Andersons' new house. If you yelled in the kitchen, you could hear your voice all over again. You could roll an orange down the counter island for ten whole seconds. I wondered, could toilet paper in one bathroom stretch to the other bathrooms? It could, just barely.

But Amanda didn't think it was funny.

"You messed up my new house," Amanda said when her mom drove me home.

"It's not a house," I told her. "My mom says it's a Mick Mansion."

After that, Mom didn't have any play dates with Mrs. Anderson, either.

But Mom didn't even notice. She's too busy sewing dresses, or sometimes she gets on the train. Dad makes dinner. She's got to keep meeting with the people at Macy's, because you never know.

4. THE ONLY CHILD

FINALLY, IT'S MY TURN. LET'S SEE . . .
what if everybody rode bikes everywhere? What if
we lived in trees? What if . . .

"Yes, Lola?" Mrs. D. says and raises her
eyebrows way up high.

All of a sudden my cheeks feel hot and my
throat feels scratchy. Maybe I'm coming down with a
deathly disease like the baboonic plague that Mom
watched on PBS. It killed lots of monkeys. I think.

I hold out my purple notebook with "cow gas,"

my last idea, crossed off. "They took all my ideas 'cause I had to go last!" My voice is choking off.

Mrs. D. takes a swig of coffee from her travel mug. "But because your turn is last, maybe you've had time to think of another idea?"

Hmmm. I think and think. Granny Coogan told me how you can turn rotten garbage into compost to help vegetables grow in your garden. That's good for Mother Earth, Granny said.

Granny is back in Texas. She's probably making compost right now. But I don't feel like using her rotten garbage idea.

All the kids are staring at me, especially that Little Miss Perfect Amanda Anderson. Why is she smiling at me? Why is she giving me the thumbs-up? What a meanie. I wish she was never, ever, ever born. Then I have it: the perfect idea.

"The Earth has TOO MANY PEOPLE," I say really loud so the kids in the back can hear. And I look right at Amanda Anderson with my meanest glare. She stops smiling. And her thumbs-up turns wobbly and sinks down to her lap. "We can all help Earth by only having ONE KID."

"Ooh, that's a good idea," Sophie says.

"Yeah, seven billion people live on planet Earth," Charlie says, "according to Yoonoo-dot-com."

And Jamal says, "The Earth faces severe food shortages because of overpopulation."

"Well, how do you like that?" I say, 'cause I'm in charge, even if I don't know what he meant. "So just have one kid, like my family."

Amanda's hand shoots up. "If you're an only child, then who's Jack?" she says, sweet as pie. Sour cherry pie.

"I didn't call on you, Amanda Anderson!" I yell back.

"Jack's your older brother, that's who!" Amanda says anyway. And she adds, "Cheater," with her sound turned down.

"It's true," says Jessie Chavez. "Jack Zuckerman is friends with my brother!"

"Raise your hand, Jessie Chavez!" I tell her. She raises her hand. But I don't call on her.

Mrs. D. comes and stands by me. "You do have a brother, don't you, Lola?" she says.

I nod. "He wrote 'Go Yankees!' all over my green notebook," I explain. "And 'Jack rules the world.'"

"But he's still your brother," she says.

I hang my head 'cause it feels like a big ol' watermelon. I stare at my watermelon-smelling pencil and my brand-new purple notebook.

Mrs. D. says, gentle as can be, "It's not a bad idea, Lola. But we all already have our sisters and brothers, don't we? Even when they write on our notebooks . . . When you're all grown-ups, you can certainly choose to have one child, or none."

Everybody laughs really loud, even me. Mrs. D. gives out THE LOOK and we stop.

"Might you have another Going Green idea, Lola? One that we could begin this September?"

I feel as sad as a "Z." Bad and mad and not at all glad. I am "Z."

My one-kid-only idea had been so good. Now I'm plumb out of ideas and I won't get to be Captain Green. And it's all Amanda Anderson's fault.

But I remember something.

"YES! I have another one!" I say to Mrs. D.

"I knew you would!" Mrs. D. sings out. "Okay, let's hear it."

"A Going Green problem is SUVs. Mom says they gulp gas," I say.

Mrs. D. smiles at me and nods. She gives me a big thumbs-up.

I keep going. "This morning we were walking to school, and somebody went speeding down the road in her SUV. That driver threw out a bunch of litter on the way. Maybe."

The smile on Mrs. D's face goes a little wilty. Mrs. D. asks, "And your solution?"

But I keep on going. "And guess what?" I say. "That SUV driver, litter-bugger is right here in our class! Her name rhymes with Ramanda Randerson."

5. SORRY, MAYBE

I HAVE TO MISS GYM, AND THAT'S my favorite class when we do relays around cones. 'Cause I am fast! *Zip, zip, zip!* I learned that from my dog, Patches.

I have to sit in the classroom all by myself, unless you count Mrs. D. at her desk grading papers and sipping coffee.

PART ONE: I have to write a note saying sorry to Amanda Anderson.

Dear Amanda Anderson,

I am sorry that I made you cry at Going Green. I hope you are having fun at gym. Cause I'm not. Too bad you decided not to wear a Lola dress. It's got secret pockets. As you know.

Sincerely,
Lola Zuckerman

PART TWO: I have to come up with ANOTHER Going Green idea, a really, really good one. 'Cause Mrs. D. knows I have it in me.

But where is it?

I wish I could ask my dad for help. Or I wish I could ask Mom. Or . . . well, not Jack; he would tell me something like the Earth is going to explode in a billion years, so who cares about Going Green. But I care a whole lot. I bet he did too when he won. Now he's old so he probably forgot. Or maybe that stinker wants to be the only Zuckerman winner!

I stare out the window. The little kindergarten

kids are blowing bubbles at their recess. I wish I was still a little kid. I turn back to my paper. It's so quiet in here. How's a person supposed to think?

Maybe I should use Granny's rotten garbage idea. She made one of those compost piles in our backyard. It stunk! Granny and I carried out coffee grounds and eggshells, and mixed them with old grass and leaves.

She and Grampy Coogan stayed in the extra room for all of June and half of July. Mom got a great opportunity to learn EVEN MORE sewing stuff in New York City. That's why Granny and Grampy came. Granny and I planted a garden full of cucumbers and tomatoes and even zucchinis. Mom sewed us matching gardening hats in her class. Grampy showed me how to do the Dead Man's Float at the town pool; and once he let Jack drive the car in the parking lot.

Jack said they were going to move in and make chocolate-chip cookies every day. But Granny said

they could only
come for six weeks.
Still, we hoped
to change her mind.
We made them
breakfast in bed
with a real rose in a
glass, and played them "Chopsticks" on the piano
'cause Granny loves piano music. We pretended to
like *The Bob Johnson News Hour* with Grampy. And we
only once played "Blanket of Doom" on the guest

bed. Even though we stayed on our best behavior, except once or twice when we fell off, they STILL went home to Texas. After they left, I got to sleep with Patches for company. And Jack got grounded. 'Cause that was a ball-face lie that Granny and Grampy couldn't take it anymore. Maybe.

The bell rings and the kids start pouring into the classroom. They're all sweaty from gym.

I sigh and write "compost." I have to use Granny's idea, 'cause I am OUT of green ideas.

Amanda comes in hand-in-hand with Jessie in their sort-of-matching polka-dotted dresses.

I look at my desk. Maybe Jessie and Amanda are talking about wearing stripes tomorrow. Or maybe they will send peanut butter up to the North Pole to glue together the polar ice caps. Or something.

Mrs. D. finishes grading papers and drinking coffee.

"Hello, Lollipops! Welcome back."

Mrs. D. gives me THE LOOK. That one means,

"Give Amanda your note."

So I walk over and give Amanda my note.
And my thumb and finger do something.
They squish that note just a little bit.
It's an accident. Maybe.

6. LAST-BUT-NOT-LEAST, LOLA

MRS. D. SITS DOWN AT HER DESK and gives me the finger. Not the one Jack gave me and got NO DESSERT for a week, the "come here" one.

I trudge to the front of the class. What if Granny Coogan is plum crazy? What if you can't turn garbage into plant food?

I clear my throat. I *clap, clap, clap-clap-clap*, just like Mrs. D., even though no one is talking.

"I heard some amazing problems today," I say. "I

heard about global warming and juice boxes."

Mrs. D. clears her throat.

I keep going. "I heard about how people want to get rid of pool heaters, even though only two people have one."

Mrs. D. says, "Lola? Where's this going?"

I cross the front of the room. Just like Mrs. D. "But I'm going to tell you about my new Going Green problem. Which," and here I point my finger across the room, "is EVERYONE'S problem. Candy Corns, that problem is garbage: garbage and lots of it!"

"Cool!" Harvey Baxter yells out.

"Okay, Lola, we're running out of time here," Mrs. D. says in her dry toast voice.

"My Mom and I walked to school to save gas and save the world from global warming," I say. "We saw a LOT of trash. We saw water bottles and banana peels and Choc Chew wrappers and Niblets wrappers and an old baby bib."

"My brother threw his sippy cup out the car window," Rita says. "I called him a litterbug and I got in trouble. It wasn't fair."

"Thank you, Rita," Mrs. D. says.

"We all make tons of trash every day. Our planet is being killed by trash!" I say.

"Amanda already said that problem!" Jessie yells. "And we could have a no-trash lunch. Problem solved!"

I squint my eyes at Jessie. "I know that. I have another solution. A better one."

"What is it, Lola?" Mrs. D. takes a sip from her travel mug.

My mouth drops open. I wish I could ask Granny. She knows lots of stuff, like how to whistle with her mouth shut. She knows how to

turn garbage into gold. That's what she said.

"Uh . . . ," I look out the window and see the custodian carrying a big bag of garbage across the yard. That gives me an idea. "Everyone should bring their garbage to school! Just for one day. We could turn it into a compost pile."

Madison's hand shoots up.

"Yes?" I say to Madison.

"What's a compost pile?" she asks.

"It's a pile of garbage that turns into good stuff."

"Like gold coins?" Sam yells out.

"Hand, Sam," I tell him.

Amanda's hand shoots up. I nod to Amanda.

"So you think we should bring our garbage to school? Like banana peels and all that stuff?"

"Yep, and we can use the compost for the community garden," I say. "That helps the vegetables grow up."

"Won't it stink?"

"Plug your nose," I say.

"Or put it in an air-tight container," Mrs. D. says. Her nose is wrinkling up like she already smells garbage.

"Well . . ." Amanda says. She looks like the ribbon in her hair is too tight.

Ari Shapiro's hand shoots up.

"Yes," I say.

"Can I bring in my sister's Pretty Cry Baby doll? That's garbage."

"No," I say. "That's plastic. It has to be something that will get rotten."

"It is rotten," Ari says.

Mrs. D. stands. "Thank you, Lola. Where did you get the idea?"

I try not to let my face get red. Was Granny crazy?

"My Granny has a compost pile in Texas," I finally say.

"Well, it's a wonderful

idea!" Mrs. D. says. "But where would we put a compost pile?"

Uh-oh.

"Yeah," Harvey yells. "Not on the playground. That would STINK!"

"*PEE-YOO!*" Jessie yells.

Then I remember something: Uncle Ken's Kitchen Composter in our garage. Granny gave it to us right before she went back to Texas so we could keep on composting even when it was snowing outside.

"We can use Uncle Ken's Kitchen Composter," I tell Mrs. D. and all those no-good yellers. "That's where you put garbage into a machine and it makes compost."

"Great problem-solving, Lola," Mrs. D. says.

On my way back to my seat I give Amanda a little smile, a sweet-as-pie smile. Lemon pie.

"Peppermints, you really did a marvelous job with this assignment. Now, before we head off to

meet up with our fifth grade buddies, write your choice on a piece of paper and your name under it."

We *scratch scratch scratch*. Mrs. D. collects our ballots. She counts them up.

We sit there like dead old carrots in a compost pile.

Finally, she is done. She has a big smile on her face.

"We have a tie," she says. "One winner is Amanda's trash-free lunch project."

I suck in my breath.

"The other winner is Lola's indoor composter."

And let it out!

"Fight! Fight! Fight!" Harvey Baxter yells.

"Harvey, we will not fight," Mrs. D. says. "We'll do another vote."

Rita raises her hand. "I'm for Lola's project. Let's make compost!"

Jessie raises her hand. "Our class will stink if we do Lola's idea."

"Compost, compost, compost!" the boys start yelling, and me and Rita.

"No trash, no trash, no trash!" the girls yell back, except me and Rita.

Clap, clap, clap-clap-clap.

"Okay, people!" Mrs. D. says. "THAT'S ENOUGH." We quiet down REAL FAST.

Mrs. D. takes a breath. "So think about what you want to vote for. No talking. No sharing with your neighbor. Think about a trash-free lunch day. That would mean packing a lunch without water bottles, throw-away plastic bags, or paper napkins. The purpose would be to produce less trash. Think about creating a compost heap. That would mean bringing in a small container of garbage. The purpose would be to turn our garbage into mulch for the community garden. Lollipops, we'll vote tomorrow!"

7. A BRILLIANT IDEA

DAD'S SHINY CAR GLIDES INTO THE garage. I run outside. Patches races me.

"Hi, Dad!" I yell. I do that every night.

"How's my Little Lola Lemon Drop?" Dad drops his briefcase and scoops me up. He always does. Patches sits on his hiney legs and whines, 'cause he wishes Dad would pick him up, too. Dad sets me down, grabs his briefcase, and I take his hand and pull him to the door.

"Dad, Mom made spaghetti and meatballs.

I'm going to use the leftovers for a compost pile."

"Oh yeah?" Dad says. "You think there'll be leftovers?"

That's a good point.

I set the table. Mom heaps spaghetti and meatballs on everyone's plates. Dad washes his hands and sits down, looking at us with a smile.

"Do I get a hello?" Dad asks Jack.

Jack's at his seat, reading *Sports Illustrated for Kids*.

"Oh, hi, Dad," he says with a metal smile. I'm not allowed to call him Brace Face, even if he likes it. He sets down his magazine and starts to eat.

I poke at my meatball. It has little green flecks in it. I take the world's smallest bite. It tastes good.

But I want to save it for my compost pile.

"I'll eat those if you don't want 'em," Jack says.

"Chew with your mouth shut," Mom tells Jack.

We go around the table and say two things about our day. Everyone else has to guess which one is true and which one is the lie. The winner gets to go next.

Dad goes first tonight. "I met the President of the United States. I finished the drawings for the new City Hall."

"You didn't meet the President!" Jack screams, and me too, but not fast enough.

"Right," Dad says with a big smile.

"My turn!" Jack says. Then he thinks. "I got back my math quiz and I got an A. I got back my math quiz and I got a C."

"You didn't get an A!" I say.

"You didn't get a C," Mom says.

"*UNNNH.*" Jack makes a buzzer sound. "Wrong, Lola! I got an A! Mom is right."

"Oh, fishsticks! You usually get a C," I say. "So that was a good guess."

"What do you mean 'fishsticks'?" Jack asks.

"That's a nice way of cursing. Grampy Coogan taught me," I explain.

"It's not fishsticks," Jack says, "it's fiddlesticks."

"No, sir. Right, Mom? It's fishsticks."

Mom shrugs. That's a cross between shut up and *ugh!* "My turn. The Kute Kids Clothing Company placed an order for four hundred Lola dresses. I won the lottery."

"Lottery!" Jack screams.

"Lottery!" I scream.

"You didn't win the lottery," Dad says.

Mom takes a deep breath. "I did!" she says. "Mrs. McCracken down the street bought me a ticket to thank me for sewing her a gardening apron. She loves the special pockets for her tools."

"Are we rich?" Jack asks. "Can I get a new bike?"

Mom shakes her head. "I won twenty-five dollars, and I split it with her."

"Why?" I say. "She's a meanie, and she hates Patches. Is it my turn?"

"She doesn't hate Patches. But she doesn't like holes in her yard," Dad says.

"Patches likes 'em," I say. "Is it my turn?"

Mom smiles. "One more thing, the Kute Kids Clothing Company did place an order for Lola dresses. Thirty-six dresses. Maybe more if they take off."

"That's great, honey," Dad says. He reaches over

and gives her a big ol' kiss and a squeezy hug.

Finally, it's my turn.

"I found a black kitten in the backyard. Actually two kittens, one black and one white," I say. "I am tied for first place with Amanda Anderson for . . ."

Jack screams over me, "Tied for first place!"

"Jack, let her finish," Dad says.

"Tied for first place in the Going Green contest, and our class is voting tomorrow," I say in one big breath.

"That one," Jack says. "That's the truth. You are?"

"That's right!" I say. "Amanda says we have to bring our lunch in reusable containers. I say we bring garbage to school, and make compost like Granny Coogan."

"Your idea sounds dumb," Jack says. "To win that Going Green contest you have to do something great. Like me. I invented unplug day. Our class unplugged six hundred and fifty-four energy-sucking plugs." He rips out a huge belch.

"That's ONE," Mom says to Jack. On three he has to go to his room. Then she says to me, "It sounds like a wonderful idea, Lola."

"What do you think, Dad?" I wait. Dad won't say he loves the idea just because he loves me.

Dad looks right at me. "Lola, I think it's brilliant."

"And could I bring the composter that Granny Coogan gave us?" I ask. "Since we never use it."

Mom looks pink. "I'm not much of a gardener."

"You are much of a cook," Jack says, spearing a meatball.

"What's that composter bin called?" Dad asks.

"The stinker," Jack says.

"Uncle Ken's Kitchen Composter," I say. "And guess what? You have to buy red wiggly worms to help make the compost. They eat the garbage and then poop it out. Then you have yourself some real nice compost. Granny Coogan said so."

"We're proud of you," Mom says.

Jack pretends that he's throwing up when Mom and Dad aren't looking.

We clean up and then Dad sets the timer. It's Quiet Reading Time In Your Room. After, it's Brownie Night.

I read, read, read. Then I come downstairs and Jack is already at the table, waiting for his brownie. And what is he wearing? His green vest! It is teensy-weensy on him. He looks like a not-Jolly-Green-Giant. I look a little closer. The gold medal pinned to it says "Green

Captain," not "Captain Green." Shucks. Harvey Baxter was right.

Jack's wearing that old green vest on purpose: to get me mad, and it's working.

"Mom! Jack's wearing his green vest just so he can brag. And it's not polite to brag. You always say so."

Jack says, "I'm not bragging. I wear this first-prize, biodegradable, recyclable, felt vest all the time. It brings back great memories: winning the Going Green contest, getting a solid gold medal, having lunch in the teacher's lounge."

I stamp my foot and Patches jumps in the air. "You do not EVER wear that vest. And you're a ball-face liar for saying that you do, 'cause you don't!"

"Lola," Mom says. "That's ONE."

Jack smiles with his metal teeth. "Yes, I do," he says all soft and sweet like an alien took him over.

I grab at Jack's green vest. "No you don't, BRACE FACE!"

He pretends to choke. "Aaaagh!" he yells.

"Lola!" Dad hollers.

"LOLA KATHERINE ZUCKERMAN!" Mom yells. Uh-oh, three names. She pulls me off Jack. "That's TWO."

"That's not fair!" I say. "He's being a trouble-maker. Not me!"

"Poor little Lola," says Jack. "Wait a second."

Jack runs upstairs. He comes back down with a teeny-tiny swimming trophy. "Here, Lola. Here's a nice shiny trophy to start your collection."

Dad raises his eyebrow. "That's thoughtful of you, but I'm sure Lola can win her own prizes."

"Maybe," Jack says, "maybe not."

"Of course she can," Mom says. "And that's TWO."

"But . . ."

"Let's not go to three," Dad says, "both of you."

I help myself to another brownie. And give Jack a smile, sweet as pie. Sour apple pie.

8. BEFORE THE BELL

IT'S *THIS* LOUD IN THE CLASSROOM.

Harvey Baxter and Sam Noonan are testing how far they can lean back in their chairs before crashing to the ground. Jamal is working on a BIG math problem on the blackboard. Dilly Chang is shrieking, "It's Going Green Day! It's Going Green Day!" Mrs. D. is standing at the door, greeting all the kids.

I decide to sharpen my watermelon-smelling pencil one more time. Madison Rogers is already there, sharpening a whole pack of pencils. I sigh.

"I like Amanda's project better," Madison says. "I'm voting for Amanda."

"I guess you don't care about making compost and growing organic vegetables," I say.

"Yes, I do!"

"I guess all you care about is eating out of reusable containers," I say, "and starving all the carrots."

"No, I don't!" Madison turns back to the sharpener and finishes up her pencils. As she passes by me, she says, "I do so care about vegetables, and fruits."

I shrug and sharpen my one, watermelon-smelling pencil. Then I spy with my little eye a double-A cheater.

Amanda Anderson is handing out chocolates to the kids in the class. She's

wearing her good-luck ribbon and her good-luck
dress. It's a Lola dress that my Mom made for her,
with a special pocket for ribbons, 'cause Amanda
Anderson loves ribbons. Why did Amanda decide
to wear that dress today?

"Hey!" I say loud and clear. "That's not fair."

Amanda turns to look at me. "Why not?"

"You're just giving them candy so they'll vote for
you."

"That's mean, Lola Zuckerman! Take that back,"
Amanda says. But her face is pink like cotton candy.

"And why are you wearing a Lola dress that my
mom made you?"

"Because," Amanda says.

"Because is not a good answer, young lady," I tell her.

"Well, I wish I wasn't!" Amanda says in her warbly old voice.

Jessie Chavez comes up and puts her arm around Amanda. "What's wrong, Amanda?"

"Nothing," Amanda says.

"You better be nice to her," Jessie says.

"You better shut your trap," I say.

Mrs. D. sings out, "Hello, people!"

Lucky for me, because my mad is about to turn into sad.

"Gummy bears! Seats, please! We have a very exciting day before us. Who can tell us what today is?" Mrs. D. sure has a bad memory.

"It's Going Green Day!" Sam shouts out.

Mrs. D. sighs and takes a drink from her travel mug. "Hand, Sam!" she reminds him.

He shoots his hand in the air.

"Yes, Sam?"

"It's Going Green Day."

I take my seat. Right in front of me, Harvey Baxter is hopping in his seat, as usual. UP, down. UP, down. I wish Mrs. D. would notice, but I don't want to be a tattletale. Like people who rhyme with Ramanda Randerson.

People who rhyme with Ramanda Randerson know all about tattling.

8½. PEOPLE WHO RHYME WITH RAMANDA RANDERSON, AND TATTLE

LAST YEAR, AT THE END OF FIRST grade, Quick and Easy Moving Company pulled into Amanda's driveway. It loaded up all her family's stuff. Amanda was moving. And I was very sad.

But at Share, Amanda told everyone about her new house, and how it was so much better than her old house. Her new house had six bathrooms and a built-in TV in the family room. And she had a new neighbor, too, named Jessie Chavez. She could get to Jessie's house anytime she wanted through the bushes.

When it was my turn to share, I told everyone that a new family was moving into Amanda's old house. I said that they had triplets who were exactly my age. I said they were building a tree fort in their

backyard for everyone on my street. And I said if you didn't live on our street, you couldn't go into the tree fort.

And guess what Jessie did? She raised her hand and said, "Where are they, then? How come they're not at school?"

I couldn't think of a good answer.

At recess I didn't swing Double Dippers with Amanda. At lunch I wouldn't share my special cookies, even though Mom had baked an "L" for Lola and an "A" for Amanda. I spelled "LA" and sang "la, la, la." Then I ate both of them.

During Circle Time, Amanda sat right next to me, even though I ate her cookie. I gave her a little pinch. Amanda yelled, "*Ow!*" and when the teacher came over, Amanda tattled on me.

The teacher said I had to say I was sorry. I really was sorry. But after that, Amanda didn't want to be my friend anymore. She said I was Jell-O, 'cause she knows I hate Jell-O. So I said she was apple pie, 'cause she told me once it tasted like slime.

We don't have any triplets on my street. That was a ball-face lie. Somebody moved in with a brand-new baby that can't play yet. We don't have Grampy and Granny Coogan anymore to do the Dead Man's Float or grow a garden.

And I will never, ever understand why everyone can't just stay put.

9. AND THE WINNER IS . . .

HARVEY BAXTER IS LEANING OFF

the side of his chair. Mrs. D. claps her hands: *clap, clap, clap-clap-clap.* "Jujubes! Now we're going to vote one last time. Please write 'compost' or 'trash-free lunch.'"

I raise my hand. "It's 'compost with Uncle Ken's Kitchen Composter.'"

Mrs. D. looks like she needs a nap. "Let's just write 'compost,'" she says.

Sam Noonan raises his hand. "What if I like

both ideas? What if I can't decide which to pick?"

Mrs. D. pauses. "You have to choose one, Sam."

He nods and writes on his piece of paper.

"Eyes on your paper, Lola," Mrs. D. says.

I write "compost" in giant letters across the page.

"I'm writing 'compost,'" Harvey Baxter loud whispers.

"Me, too," Sam says.

I look over at Amanda right between Harvey and Sam. Her eyes shine up. Her cheeks get all rosy, even her ears. Poor Amanda.

I remember one time in kindergarten when I opened my lunchbox and there was nothing in there 'cause Mom forgot to pack it. My eyes loaded up with tears. But before I could let 'em go, Amanda stuck half of her peanut-butter-and-jelly sandwich right in my mouth! And Amanda gave me half of everything ELSE she had. We had half of some baby carrots, half of an orange, and half of a Swiss chocolate. We even ripped Mrs. Anderson's I

LOVE YOU note in half. I said, "Why did you share EVERYTHING with me?" And she said, "'Cause you're Lola, and plus you're my best friend." That's when we invented the secret Peanut Butter and Jelly handshake, which I can't talk about because it's secret.

I have a hard time making my hand erase "compost." But finally it does and I write "trash-free lunch"—small but clear—instead. Mrs. D. goes around the room and collects the scraps of paper.

"Does anyone remember what these papers are called?" she asks.

"Baldos?" Rita says.

"Banjos?" Sam guesses.

"I don't get it," Harvey Baxter says.

"Because you like stinky trash," Jessie Chavez whispers from behind me. Except I hear that mean-o.

Fishsticks! Why did I vote for Amanda Anderson?

"Ballots!" Miss Smarty-Pants Amanda Anderson says.

Mrs. D. says, "That's right, Amanda! A ballot is your vote. It's the written form of your vote."

"It comes from *ballotta*, the Italian word for ball," Jamal says, "because people used to vote with colored balls."

"In Finland, we're a social democracy. That's different than America," says Timo.

"Do you get to vote in Finland?" I ask.

"No, I'm too young," Timo says.

"Luckily you get to vote here," I say with my biggest smile. My brother says it makes me look like a hyena, but I think I look like the President.

Amanda makes her eyes really big and she smiles at Timo, too. "That's right, Timo. Vote for the BEST choice."

Mrs. D. takes my ballot. It's too late to take back my vote.

Finally, Mrs. D. has all the ballots. "Uh-oh, we have an even number of kids at school today. If nine kids vote for compost and nine kids vote for trash-free lunch . . . we could have a tie."

The door bangs open. It's Gwendolyn Swanson-Carmichael.

"Sorry I'm late," she says, and then *boom!* She

trips over her own foot and drops all her books.

"Let me help you!" I smack my purple notebook down and run to help Gwendolyn.

"Thanks, Lila," she says. That Gwendolyn always gets my name wrong. But I'll remind her that I'm L-O-L-A later on, after she votes.

"Me too, Gwendolyn," Amanda says and dives to the floor. We both grab Gwendolyn's Writer's Workshop notebook.

"Gimme that," I say. I try to pry off Amanda's pinky finger. Then I remember that I better not bend back her fingers or Miss Cry Baby will tattle on me AGAIN. "Here you go, Gwendolyn," I say as sweet as a packet of sugar. I hand over her books.

You can guess what that copycat Amanda does.

"You're just in time," Mrs. D. says to Gwendolyn. "We just voted for the Going Green project. Write down your vote on a piece paper."

"And it could be a tie AGAIN!" Harvey Baxter yells.

"Then hers will be the swing vote," Jamal says.

Harvey Baxter says, "What's a swing vote?"

"It's the vote that swings the election one way," Jamal points to Amanda, who smiles. Jamal points to me. "Or another; if nine votes are for Amanda and nine votes are for Lola, then Gwendolyn's vote will make one of them win."

"I bet she came in late to be a swinger," Sam says.

"Hand, Sam," Mrs. D. says. She takes Gwendolyn's ballot. She counts.

My stomach feels like a compost machine.

"I have a winner," Mrs. D. says quietly.

The class sucks in its breath.

"The winner is Lola's compost idea."

Amanda bursts into tears and runs from the room.

I feel terrible. Seventy-five percent terrible and twenty-five percent not so bad.

10. OLD SPINACH

AFTER RECESS, MRS. D. GIVES ME the Green Vest. It's the MOST WONDROUS thing you ever saw or did see or have seen. It's made of green one-hundred percent recycled wool, and it has a gold badge on it that says "Green Captain."

I get to have lunch with Mrs. D. in the TEACHER'S LOUNGE. I bring my sack lunch with me, just in case. But my mouth is all set for candy. I do my special walk-skip to get there quick. But Mrs. D. walks SO slowly. It takes us about four-hundred hours just to make it down the hall.

Finally we get inside that teacher's lounge and guess what? NO CANDY! Those teachers hid it, I bet. It smells like Grampy's coffee breath mint breath in there, too.

There's just a big table and somebody wrote "HELP" in ink on it! And a coffee machine with a sign taped on the wall behind it that says "I live for coffee!" There's a yellow couch where Mrs. Graham is eating yogurt with her shoes off, and some arm chairs, oh, and a fridge. Mr. Carp is filling up his coffee cup and Mrs. D. gets in line to fill up her mug. While she's up there, I look around for chocolate. No chocolate, nothing. Maybe she keeps it under the table.

I'm crawling under the table when Mrs. D.'s shoes walk up. Then her face comes down. "What are you doing, Lola?"

"Looking for chocolate," I explain.

"Lola . . . why on earth do you think you'd

find chocolate under the table?"

I scooch on out of there. "Jack told me the teacher's lounge is one-hundred percent candy," I say. "I'm guessing that's a ball-face lie."

Mrs. D.'s mouth twitches. "I'm afraid so, Lola. Why don't we sit down and eat our lunch?" She takes out a spinach salad with croutons. She chomps her salad. I take out my bagel. But I'm too mad and sad to eat it.

Mrs. D. puts her fork down and puts her hand on mine. "Lola, Jack told you a tall tale, didn't he?"

"He told me a whopper," I say.

Mrs. D. smiles at me. "That's a problem, isn't it?"

She wants me to be a problem-solver. I can just tell. "But I can't solve this problem, Mrs. D.," I say wistfully. Wistfully is a cross between wishing for something and getting mist in your eyes when you don't have it. "I can't make it one-hundred percent candy in here."

Mrs. D. looks around. And guess what? She looks wistful, too. 'Cause I guess she'd like to eat fudge for lunch instead of spinach.

"No," she says. "But next time Jack—or anyone—tells you something that seems too good to be true, you might wonder about it."

"I don't like that," I tell her. "I

want to believe in stuff that's too good to be true."

Mrs. D. nods. "What if the teacher's lounge was one percent candy?"

"That would be good. Not too good, either," I say, "just the right amount of good."

"Let's finish our lunch and see about that one percent," she says. "Agree?"

"I agree," I say and take a big bite out of my bagel. Because I'm getting hungry!

While we eat, I tell her all about how worms eat garbage for lunch and their poop makes compost and compost makes vegetables grow.

"Who taught you so much about composting?" Mrs. D. asks. "Your mom or dad?"

"Granny Coogan," I explain. And my wistful feeling comes back a little because I miss her and I wish she was in the guest bedroom taking a nap.

We finish up and Mrs. D. reaches into the fridge and pulls out a giant box. We sit down and open the lid and inside I see CHOCOLATE, all kinds of

chocolate; dark and light and white and square and round. And Mrs. D. and I each take one. We eat our chocolate together.

Then we go back to class and I feel sweet and soft as milk chocolate, and I wish I could give one piece of chocolate to Amanda. In Writer's Workshop, I write a story about a possum that's mean to her best friend.

After lunch, it's time for the class to talk about how we're going to compost. Amanda's eyes are still red, and so is her nose. I try to get hold of her eyes with my eyes. But she won't look at me. I wish she would so I could smile, even if she did move way far away from me, right snuggled up next to Jessie Chavez. I want to tell her I voted for her project, but probably she wouldn't believe me.

Mrs. D. stands at the blackboard with a big piece of chalk. "Gumdrops, think about what we can put in our compost pile. Let's brainstorm!" That's when kids make it rain ideas inside their brains.

Dilly Chang raises her hand. "Is old spinach good

for our pile? We have some left over."

Mrs. D. looks at me. "Lola?"

"Great!" I say. "That's green food."

Mrs. D. writes it down.

Harvey Baxter raises his hand.

"I ate spinach once. Then I threw it up."

Mrs. D. nods. "Thank you, Harvey. You may put your arm down."

"How about moldy bread?" Ari Shapiro asks.

Hmm. "I think so," I say. It's hard to be an expert

right away. Mrs. D. writes it down, so maybe I'm right.

Amanda raises her hand. "What if we all of a sudden get allergic to mold?"

"That's possible," Mrs. D. says. She drops her chalk and bends down to get it.

Amanda turns back and sticks her tongue out at me.

Mrs. D. stands up. "But not likely," she says.

Amanda puts her tongue back in.

Jessie Chavez's hand shoots up. "Mrs. D., what if we eat out all the time and we don't have garbage?"

"Ask for a doggy bag," she says.

"We also need some people to bring in brown things," I say. "'Cause we need one part brown things and two parts green things."

"Brown things like mud?" Gwendolyn Swanson-Carmichael asks.

"Or burnt oatmeal-raisin cookies?" Ruby Snow asks.

"Or old sneakers?" Jessie Chavez asks.

"How 'bout my mom's casserole?" Ruby asks. "It's dark brown." She makes a yuck face.

"No, it's got to be straw, twigs, or leaves," I say.

"How about dirty diapers?" Sophie Nunez asks. "They're brown."

"NO WAY!" the whole class shouts.

"Fluffernutters," Mrs. D. says, "tomorrow

morning, please bring your garbage in a sealed bag. A through H, please bring in something from Lola's brown garbage list. I through Z, please bring in something from the green list."

"This is the stinkiest idea I ever heard," Amanda Anderson says when we line up for dismissal. "Nobody's going to bring any garbage. Who would want to stink up the class?"

"Not me, that's for sure!" Jessie shoots out.

Mrs. D. is busy with hand-outs. She doesn't hear. But I do. I hear mean ol' sore-loser Amanda Anderson loud and clear.

Fishsticks.

How come if I'm a winner I feel bad?

11. WOO WHEE, BOYS!

"I WON!" I YELL WHEN I HOP OFF the bus after school. Patches barks and Mom says "hip hip hooray." In olden days that meant "yay."

Mom hugs me four hundred times and we do a green captain dance in the kitchen. She twirls around her measuring tape. Patches goes wild. "We'll have to call Granny Coogan," Mom says. "She'll be so proud that she inspired your idea."

Fishsticks! If Granny Coogan stayed put in the extra room, she would already know all about it.

I see my brother the ball-face candy liar crashing through the door.

"Guess what?" Jack says. "My homeroom teacher gave me the Good Apple award. It was for being a caring citizen. I carried my friend Mike's backpack for two solid weeks 'cause he's on crutches."

"That's wonderful, Jack!" Mom says. Her voice sounds all choky. "Just wait until Dad sees that. Oh, honey, he'll be SO proud."

"And he'll be proud that I won the Going Green contest," I say loud and clear. I wait for Mom to say, "Yes, Dad will be SO, SO, SO proud of you. That mean ol' Amanda Anderson is WRONG. Everyone will love to bring in their garbage." But the phone rings. Mom answers it. "Oh, hi,

BLAH
BLAH

Mom," she says and gives a big smile. She forgot that Granny Coogan can't see her. "Is that right?" she says. And then, "Well, I heard, blah, blah, blah."

I wait and wait and wait for her to say, "GUESS WHAT? LOLA IS THE WINNER OF THE GOING GREEN CONTEST."

But she keeps saying dumb stuff.

I stomp over to the garbage can and find NO GARBAGE for Uncle Ken's Kitchen Composter.

I yell, "Mom, where's the garbage?"

Mom covers the phone with her hand. She gives me a MEAN look. "Lola, I am on the phone." I always don't like "on the phone," but now I really hate "on the phone."

"Please be patient," she says.

Being patient means you have to act like you're in the hospital and you're really sick and tired. You have to wait and wait and act like you have all the time in the world.

Finally Mom gets off the phone. She looks at me

and then claps herself right on the head. "Oh, Lola, I completely forgot to tell Granny about your green project."

"Never mind," I say. "I don't even care one bit."

"But Granny would love . . ."

"Where's all the garbage, Mom?"

"I guess the garbage man came and took our garbage today," she says. "Why? Did you want it?"

"HOW COULD YOU DO THAT? YOU JUST RUINED THE EARTH AND MY PROJECT!" I holler.

"That's ONE." And she means I get a punishment, not herself for throwing out the golden garbage.

"Come on," Jack says. "Let's go play Blanket of Doom on the guest bed."

I bet Jack wants to be a

Good Apple again and get me out of Mom's hair.

"No roughhousing," Mom says. "Remember? You broke Granny's reading glasses playing that game."

"How about Jungle Tracker," Jack says.

"Only if you're the antelope," I say.

"Fine." And we bang out to the backyard.

At dinner, Dad is proud of me for winning the Going Green contest. But he talks way more about Jack winning the stinky Good Apple award.

I put my school bag by my chair. When nobody is looking, I wrap up two pieces of garlic bread and slide them in my school bag. They will be perfect for Uncle Ken's Kitchen Composter. Except somebody was looking, Mom, and Mom says, "That's TWO, Lola." I put the garlic bread back.

Mom takes the lid off the russell sprouts. Russell sprouts are green stink balls.

When something stinks, Granny Coogan says, "WOO WHEE, BOYS!" and plugs her nose.

"WOO WHEE, BOYS!" I say and plug my nose. "That smells like garbage!"

"That's THREE, Lola," Dad says. "Go to your room, please."

"What a dummy," Jack says.

"That's ONE, Jack," Mom says.

Mom and Dad look like it's past their bedtime.

I grab my school bag and stomp up to my room, *BAM! BAM! BAM!*, 'cause there's only three and go to your room. You can be as bad as you want on the way. You sit there and think about how mean your mom and dad are, and then you come out and say sorry.

I can hear Jack talking in a funny voice downstairs, and Dad is laughing.

I look out my window. Maybe I could make a sheet rope and climb out the window and run away. I could go to a family that really appreciates mulch.

I open my door a crack. The coast is clear. I creep down the stairs and into the kitchen. I can hear

Mom and Dad and Jack in
the family room watching
a baseball game on TV.
"Hey, he caught a ball
with his left hand just like
you did at your last game,
Jack," Mom says.

"I need to build you
a special trophy shelf
this weekend," Dad says,
"for all your awards and
trophies."

A special trophy shelf?
Fishsticks!

I look into the garbage
can. Sure enough, there are leftovers from dinner.
They sure do smell . . . garbage-y.

Then I see it on the kitchen table, Jack's jumbo
Good Apple trophy, and Jack's big basket of
Macintosh apples. . . . I'll eat them up and get apple

cores! That's the perfect garbage. Those Macintosh apples are Amanda's favorites. Maybe I should save her one. No, I won't. Jessie Chavez can go win a Good Apple award.

Mom and Dad won't care if I take a few apples or a bunch. Maybe. Even though they're part of Jack's prize, 'cause an apple a day keeps the doctor away. So a bunch of apples will keep a bunch of doctors away.

I huff the basket upstairs to my room and take off the plastic. I eat the first apple. But then I just take a bite out of all the rest. I bite, bite, bite all the apples.

When I'm done, I'm stuffed full of apples.

And I have a WHOLE lot of garbage.

I stuff all the apple cores in the plastic from the basket. I stuff the whole thing into my school bag.

And I stuff myself in bed.

And I'm lying there stuffed up and the phone rings.

And Mom comes into the room and she whispers, "Lola?"

But I squeeze my eyes shut.

"Sorry, Mom," Mom whispers to Granny Coogan, "she's out like a light."

12. FOOD FIGHT!

I'M **TOO, TOO** EXCITED TO WAIT FOR
the bus. Plus Dad has to give me a ride on account
of my Uncle Ken's Kitchen Composter. I'm UP and
DOWN and THIS WAY and THAT WAY and OOGA
BOOGA WOOGA at breakfast. I have on my green
captain vest, and I probably won't want to take it
off, ever, ever, ever!

It would be the happiest day, except for one
thing: Jack.

"Patches, I hate you. You dumb dog, you ate all

my apples!" Jack stomps and whomps around the kitchen.

"Patches didn't mean to, I bet," I say. Poor Patches. I stuck one apple core in his dog bed this morning, and the ribbon from the basket in his toy box.

"But what happened to the basket?" Dad asks.

"Maybe he buried it," I say, even though I buried it under my bed.

"We had better keep a close watch on him,"

Mom says. "All those apples can't be good for him."

"Is Patches going to be okay?" Jack asks. All of a sudden he looks worried, just like he did when I fell out of the tree.

"He'll be fine," Dad says, "just a little stomach trouble, most likely."

Poor Patches. He has to stay out in the yard. I wave to him through the window and say "SORRY" with my sound turned off.

"Yeah, he'll be fine," I say.

At school Mrs. D. and I set up Uncle Ken's Kitchen Composter in the back of the class. It has a bunch of drawers. The worms start out in the bottom drawer and eat their way to the top.

Mrs. D. has to run back to the teacher's lounge to fill up her travel mug, and probably get some chocolate from the fridge. So Miss Nimby, the teacher's aide, is in charge till she gets back.

"Don't worry about a thing," I tell her. "I'll keep everyone busy."

It turns out EVERYBODY brought garbage! Even that double-A sore loser pants Amanda. I didn't have to eat all those apples and make a bad smell in my room from apple gas.

Even though Mrs. D. is still in the lounge getting

coffee and candy, I'm sure she won't mind if we get it all started. Maybe. And Miss Nimby looks busy erasing the board.

I unwrap my apple cores and drop them into Uncle Ken's Kitchen Composter. There are lots of trays to slide in your garbage.

"One part brown and two parts green!" I shout. "So don't forget A to H brown and I to Z green."

Dilly Chang hollers, "Here comes some bones!" She throws in twigs.

"Incoming!" Sam plops in egg shells.

"*Chugga chugga CHOO-CHOO!*" John Carmine Tabanelli chugs in some orange peels.

"Bombs away!" Harvey Baxter hollers. He tosses in some leaves.

"Here's some dead hands!" Sophie Nunez waves around some black slimy banana peels.

"Get 'em away!" Jessie screams.

Everybody takes a turn with the stinking rotten garbage.

Amanda Anderson drops in exactly one stick. Just then Mrs. D. comes rushing through the door. "Sweet Tarts!" she says. "Everyone take a seat! Who said it was time to begin?" Uh-oh. Mrs. D. gives Miss Nimby a sour milk look.

"Lola!" everyone yells.

Miss Nimby scoots out the door to help in another class.

"Lola," Mrs. D. says, "please take a seat."

"Mrs. D." Amanda says. "I only threw my stick in 'cause my mom said I had to, even though Lola's idea is weird."

126

"It's not weird! You're weird!"
I say.

"Hey!" Amanda yells.
She's pointing at Uncle Ken's
Kitchen Composter. "It says
here it'll take two whole weeks
before we even get compost! See,
it's a dumb idea."

"That will be enough from you two," Mrs. D. says.
"In my classroom, I expect everyone to give each
other CPR. Courtesy, patience, and . . ."

"RESPECT!" everyone shouts.

"Mrs. D., I am sorry," I say in my
most respectful voice. "And I have
a surprise," I say. "I got these
from Gump's Garden Supplies.
They rode home in the trunk."
I reach into my school bag
and pull out my surprise. It's a
clear plastic bag with air holes.

Inside is a heap of worms, squirming around.

Mrs. D. makes a sound like a cross between a scream and a gulp. She backs away.

"Lola!" Mrs. D. says. "Why did you bring worms to class?"

"Remember? I told you how wiggly red worms eat garbage and poop dirt. They go inside Uncle Ken's Kitchen Composter to help make compost," I re-explain.

"COOL!" Sam yells.

Mrs. D. looks funny, greenish funny.

"I don't know about those worms, Lola."

"But they'll make the garbage turn into compost faster!" I tell her. In case she forgot from two seconds ago.

"All right, did you read the directions about where they go?"

I nod. "They go on the bottom tray. On account of worms, they always climb up."

Mrs. D. shudders. "Just be sure they don't get loose." She leans down and whispers in my ear, "To tell the truth, I'm a little afraid of worms. My brother used to drop them down my shirt."

"Oh," I whisper, too. "I understand about brothers." She winks at me. And I wink back. And Mrs. D. hurries off to her desk.

At lunch I eat far away from Amanda. Sam eats the cheese slices from my cheese sandwich, and I eat his green grapes, and Sophie Nunez tells a joke about an actor who can't remember his lines, and it's really funny and milk comes out of my nose. I finish my breadwich and eat my "L" cookie. I throw my plastic baggies into the garbage.

I look into the trash can at all the plastic stuff that can't be composted.

And then I think, two whole weeks before we get any compost at all.

Maybe we should have done Amanda's idea.

Just then Amanda walks up and throws her milk carton into the garbage. Milk sprays all over me.

"Oops," Amanda says, sweet as pie. Lemon pie. "Too bad I didn't have that milk in a thermos. That would be a trash-free lunch."

"Yeah, too bad!" I reach into the garbage can and pull out a juice box. Someone has already finished half. I squeeze it hard, right in Amanda's direction. Amanda ducks, just as Gwendolyn Swanson-Carmichael is coming up to empty her Smack O Roni 'N Cheese into the trash. Amanda rams into her. The juice squirts Gwendolyn all over her face. It drips from her glasses and dribbles down her chin.

"Lola!" Gwendolyn hollers. She throws her Smack O Roni 'N Cheese right at me. Luckily, I see it coming. I dip. *SPLAT!* Ewwww. Cold cheesy noodles dribble down Ben Wexler's face.

"I'll get you for that, Gwendolyn!" Ben yells. He throws his butterscotch pudding cup right at her.

Gwendolyn screams and takes off, running right into Jamal. *BAM!* Jamal's tray flips up and his dessert splatters all over him.

"Oh, no!" Jamal moans. "That was the last butterscotch pudding." He dips his finger into the mess slithering down his shirt. "Mmmm . . . still good."

Food is flying everywhere, juice and cookies and lasagna and garlic

bread, pizza and bagels and chocolate milk and turkey slices.

TWEET! The lunch ladies blast their whistles. *TWEET!*

But no one listens.

Principal McCoy comes running into the cafeteria. He slides on a pool of chocolate milk and skids right off his feet. *BOOM!* He lands flat on his back with a *crack, crack, crack.*

Uh-oh!

"She started it!" Amanda Anderson bellows. She points right at me.

"She started it!" I bellow at the exact same time. And I point at the no-good apple-pie sore-loser stinker who rhymes with Pamanda Panderson.

12½. DEAR PRINCIPAL MCCOY

Dear Principal McCoy,

I am very sorry for throwing food and milk. I promise never ever to do that again. Not even if SOMEONE else started it and it wasn't my fault. And you'd never guess who that SOMEONE was cause she's a ball-face sore loser.

I hope your elbow feels better soon from where you fell down in the cafeteria.

Sincerely your admirer,

Lola Zuckerman

Dear Principal McCoy,

I am so so sorry that I misbehaved myself in the cafeteria. I got under a bad influence. A really bad one. You got let down by me. Right onto the floor. I hope you get those stains out.

I never have gotten in trouble, except when I get under a bad influence. From now on, I am going to be good. I will be so so good.

Yours truly,
Amanda Anderson

Dear Lola,

I wasn't there cause I had lunch detention. But I'm sorry I missed it. I bet you looked funny with milk all over your face.

Your pal,

Harvey Baxter

13. SORRY!

THE NEXT DAY EVERYBODY SAYS sorry to the head custodian, Mrs. Susanna Duff; and the lunch ladies, Pat, Tiny, and Amaryllis. After that, it is Silent Lunch. Nobody can say a word. Everybody blames me and Amanda Anderson.

Harvey Baxter gets a lunch detention all over again for passing me a smart-alecky note.

Principal McCoy wears a sling to school to hold up his sore elbow. He gives a talk in the auditorium about The Grasshopper That Threw

Food and The Ant Who Didn't Throw Her Food, but Saved It for a Rainy Day.

Sam yells out, "And don't forget The Worm That Ate Garbage and Pooped out Dirt."

He goes to sit in the hall.

Gwendolyn Swanson-Carmichael raises her hand. "I can't believe he——" she starts to say.

"Put your hand down!" Principal McCoy says, really mean. Gwendolyn Swanson-Carmichael's lips squish up.

"This is all Amanda Anderson's fault," some kid yells out.

"It's Lola Zuckerman's fault," someone else yells.

Well, maybe.

Amanda is used to being good, and she's not used to being bad. Amanda Anderson zips out of the auditorium crying. As she runs past me, she says, "I hate you, Lola! And I always will."

And I am sad, tears-coming-out sad.

In the classroom, everyone is quiet. Nobody

even wants to check on the worms in the compost bin.

Mrs. D. says, "I'm very disappointed, class." We're not Jellybeans or Jujubes or Lemon Heads. We're not even People. We're just Class.

At home I run up to my room. I shut the door and flop onto my bed. I remember me and Amanda throwing all my blankets straight out that window and into a tree. We were making a hotel for chilly squirrels. Why can't we be friends again?

● ● ●

Friday morning Mom wakes me up early. "It's Granny," she says and hands me the phone.

"Hi, Granny," I say in a cold toast voice.

"Oh, my sweet little Lola," Granny says.

"Grampy and I have been hooting and hollering down here. We're so proud of you! You won the contest. That's wunnerful!"

"Thank you, Granny," I say.

"It tickles me pink that you're teaching your friends to make compost," Granny says. "Maybe they'll start up their own gardens, just like we did."

I breathe into the phone.

"Lola? What's wrong, sweetheart? Cat got your tongue?"

"You missed seeing the zucchini get big," I say. I don't hear anything out of the phone. "Granny, are you still there?"

"Why, yes I am, Lola Lou. And you're right. We had to leave before it was time to pick the zucchini. That was a shame. Your mom told me the zucchini grew real nice. She told me you love zucchini soufflé."

My voice wobbles like Jell-O. "Jack said you and Grampy were moving in for keeps. But then you left because you couldn't take it anymore."

And you know what that Granny did? She laughed. "Oh, Lola," she said. "I wish I could stay

there forever; Grampy, too. But we had to go home."

"Because of your compost pile?" I ask.

"Well, yes, and our garden and our home, and all those cats that visit us," Granny says.

"Jenkins and Peter and Moe?" I ask.

"Yes and a few more. But Lola Lou, we loved visiting you and Jack and your mom and dad, every minute."

"Even when me and Jack played Blanket of Doom on the guest bed and broke your spare glasses?" I ask.

"Even then. I never liked those glasses much anyway," Granny says.

I take a deep breath 'cause I was running out of air. "I love you, Granny."

"I love you too, very much; you and Jack, that little stinker," Granny says.

"And Patches too?" I ask.

"Patches, too. Why, Lola, did you know that I have a picture on my fridge of you and me in the garden in our matching hats?" Granny says.

"You do?" I ask.

"Sure I do! Every time I walk by, I say, 'Hello, Lola Lou!'"

I think about that for a while. Then I say, "Granny? Does Grampy say 'fishsticks' or 'fiddlesticks'?"

"Why, 'fiddlesticks,' I suppose."

Shucks. Jack was right. Well, I like "fishsticks."

After Granny and I hang up, I feel a little better, but not a lot. I still wish I I didn't have to go to school.

But Mom takes my temperature and feels my glands. "You're fine," she says.

"No, I'm not," I say. "I'm heartsick."

"Well, why are you heartsick?" Mom's forehead wrinkles up.

"'Cause Jack's the best, and I'm the second best." Mom's mouth drops open. I can see her fillings.

"Lola!" she cries. "Whatever gave you that idea?"

"I eez-dropped on you," I say.

"Eavesdropped? When?" Mom asks.

And so I told her that I heard her talking to Dad about building a special shelf for all of Jack's awards.

"Jack's award-winning, and I'm not." And as fast as I can, I get out the hot words burning me up. "And I ate all of Jack's Good Apple apples, not Patches! I'm sorry!"

Mom sits up straight. "Lola!" she says. "Well, it's Jack you need to say sorry to."

I gulp some air. "Okay."

"And . . ." she says.

"I should buy him a bunch of apples with my birthday dollars that Granny gave me." I reach under my bed and pull out the basket. "And stick 'em in here."

Mom nods firm-like. "Good plan, Lola." Then she smiles and I know she doesn't hate me. She hugs me up. She says, "Oh, Lola, it's not fair that some kids get a lot of awards and some kids don't. But Dad and I love you just the same, awards or no awards."

My lips are all blubbery. "Okay. But I still wish I had a special trophy shelf for my green captain vest."

"I think that's a wonderful idea." Then Mom

kisses me all over my face five hundred times, and I laugh.

"But my heart is still sick," I say.

Mom takes a sigh-gulp of her coffee. "Why?"

"Because Amanda hates me," I say.

And I tell her the whole story, about zooming toilet paper through Amanda's Mick Mansion, and telling Mrs. Anderson that it WAS a Mick Mansion because Mom said that. And Mom's face gets as pink as pink roses.

"Mom," I say in a voice that even I can barely hear. "I should tell Amanda I'm sorry for running toilet paper around her house."

"And I need to tell Penny Anderson I'm sorry for calling her lovely new home a McMansion."

We drive over to Windy Hill Drive. Mom rings the bell. It makes a fancy sound.

Mrs. Anderson answers the door. She isn't smiling.

Mom sighs. "Penny, I'm here to apologize for

my unkind words. You have a beautiful new home. I never should have called it a McMansion. I think I was jealous! And life has gotten so busy with my Lola dress company."

I can't believe Mom said all those words.

Mrs. Anderson's face unpinches, and she hugs Mom. "It's okay! I'm so proud of your dress company. Amanda loves her Lola dress! She uses her special pocket for her hair ribbons. I miss Cherry Tree Lane and you!"

I don't blame her. It's REALLY quiet in the Mick Mansion, and big. I would tie a rope to the front door if I lived there so I wouldn't get lost.

Amanda comes running. "Stop being mean to my mommy!" she yells at my mom.

"She wasn't being mean!" I yell back.

"Girls!" the moms say.

"Lola," Mom says, "didn't you tell me there was something you'd like to say?"

I look at the floor. I wish I had my watermelon-smelling pencil to write my sorries.

Fishsticks! I WAS going to say sorry before Amanda came yelling at me.

I look at Amanda straight in her blue eyes. "I'm sorry for running toilet paper through your house, and other stuff, too." But I don't feel sorry.

Amanda says, "I'm sorry for milking you in the cafeteria." But she doesn't sound sorry.

"I'm sorry for juicing you back," I say. My eyes go squinty.

Amanda looks as sour as a pickle. She says, "Oh, yeah? Well, I'm sorry I lifted the top off the composting bin so the worms would run away."

Then she stops, and claps her hand on her mouth.

I just stare at that ol' Amanda Anderson.

"Amanda Susannah Anderson!" Mrs. Anderson yells. "How could you!"

I can't believe it! Miss Perfect Amanda Anderson NEVER does anything bad, except she did. And that makes me smile. Maybe even when you move to a mansion, you might still get frisky and bad. So maybe we could still be friends, mostly good but sometimes frisky and bad.

Then I remember something, something worse than plain bad.

"We've got to get to school before Mrs. D. gets there! She's afraid of worms!" I yell. "She's going to have her heart attack her if she sees a worm!"

14. THE RUNAWAYS

ME AND AMANDA AND MOM HOP into Mrs. Anderson's SUV. We zoom to school. Mrs. Anderson pulls up to the entrance, and we jump out and wave goodbye. Here come the buses.

"We've got to hurry!" I yell. We whiz inside.

We zip by Mr. Carp wheeling a cart of books into the library.

"Girls, slow down, blah, blah, blah . . ."

We are going too fast to hear.

We run into our classroom.

AAAAAGGHHH!

AAAAAGGHHH!

There is Mrs. D. standing in the middle of the room. She is throwing candy at Uncle Ken's Kitchen Composter.

Red worms are coming out of Uncle Ken's Kitchen Composter. They're wiggling on the floor.

"Worms!" Mrs. D. screams. "Give me a rat! Give me a mouse! Give me a spider or even a cockroach. I can handle it. But not worms!"

"Don't worry, Mrs. D. Save your candy!" I yell. "Amanda and I are here. We'll rescue you."

Amanda and I start picking up worms and carrying them back to the compost bin.

"Poor little worms," Amanda says. "I bet they were scared out on the carpet."

I have a bunch in my hand. "You like the worms?"

"Sure!" Amanda says. "Like you said, they eat our garbage. That's cool!"

"I like your Going Green project better," I say. Then I cross my fingers behind my back.

Amanda looks at me hard. "Really?"

"I liked it almost the same," I say.

"Your idea was better," Amanda says. Her mouth squishes.

"No, sir, it wasn't. We both had good ideas for Going Green."

Amanda looks up. "Honest?"

"I even voted for yours." I say.

"No crossies?" she asks.

I hold up my hands. "See? No

crossies. Did you vote for mine?"

Amanda nods. "Yes." Then she gets pink as Yowza gum. "Actually, no."

At first that mad bumblebee feeling comes back. *BUZZ!*

But then I remember. I voted for Amanda. Amanda voted for Amanda. And I still won.

And that makes me think of something . . . something big. Even though I am last, I am not least. 'Cause when all the ideas get taken, that's when you really have to get thinking. Maybe I'm even glad to be "Z" for zippers, zebras, and zeros; "Z" for Zuckerman. And I feel warm and melty, just like a pat of butter on a stack of hot pancakes.

"Are you mad?" Amanda asks.

"Nope." And I really wasn't. "Are you?"

"Nope."

Me and Amanda do Super Goofer Smiles. We do our secret Peanut Butter and Jelly handshake. Then we get back to work.

We get most of the worms cleaned up, but not before Gwendolyn Swanson-Carmichael arrives.

"This is outrageous!" she screams.

"Calm down," Mrs. D. says. "There are just a few worms here. They won't kill you."

"I would NEVER stand for this!" Gwendolyn says. "If I were the teacher . . ."

Mrs. D. says, "Gwendolyn, dear, would

you please stand in the hallway until the girls are finished? Tell the other kids to wait."

Finally I scoop up the last worm.

"There you go, Wormy Junior." I put him inside the compost bin right on top of an eggshell. "That's the last one, Mrs. D."

"Lola!" Amanda says. She points into the muck. "Look!"

I look. I don't see anything.

"Right there, that garbage is looking a lot like mulch."

"You're right." It's still just garbage. But that sure is nice of Amanda!

We jump around and around, holding hands. "We're Going Green! We're Going Green!"

The rest of the class comes in.

"Why did we have to wait outside?" Harvey Baxter asks.

"Just you never mind," Mrs. D. says. She's smoothing down her shirt. "Gummy worms, it's time for Share."

We all sit down on Mrs. D.'s red carpet.

Amanda Anderson says, "Our garbage pile is going to turn into food for a garden in only two weeks!" She smiles at me and I smile at her.

Harvey Baxter looks sad. "I told my parents about Going Green and they said maybe we should sell our SUV. It has a TV and I watch *Robot Rage* on it."

Jessie Chavez says in her TV commercial voice, "My mom bought me all new recyclable containers so I can have a trash-free lunch!" She grins at Amanda. "I just LOVE a trash-free lunch. Everyone should try a recyclable container today! They're on sale for a low, low—"

"Thank you, Jessie," Mrs. D. interrupts.

Everyone shares, and I am last, last, last. But I don't mind, because going last means I have lots of time to think about stuff, like how to be a friend. Because to have a friend, you have to be a friend.

And I need a lot of time to think about that one.

Last, but not least, it's my turn.

I say, "We should have two winners of Going Green: me *and* Amanda."

"Amanda and me," Mrs. D. says.

"But you didn't enter the contest," I say.

"I mean you and Amanda."

"That's what I said!" I say.

"Lola, I mean that when we speak proper English, we say the other person's name first. So please say, 'Amanda and me,' not 'me and Amanda.'"

Fishsticks. That means that Amanda gets to go first even in proper English.

"Two winners, please! Amanda and me!" I say.

Mrs. D. nods. Amanda gets all pink like Wubba Dubba Bubba gum. And I feel Z–plus, zesty, zippy, zinger, Zuckerman.

Ari Shapiro points at Mrs. D.'s lap. "Look, one got out."

Mrs. D. jumps up. "Help!" she yells. The worm flies through the air. I catch it.

"She won't hurt you," I say. "She just wants to eat garbage."

I carry the runaway worm back to the compost bin.

"But she can't eat plastic wrap. Or juice boxes. So that's why we should have Amanda's idea, too, trash-free lunches!"

"I like juice," Dilly Chang says.

"You can drink it. Just bring it in a thermos," Amanda says, "or a stainless-steel water bottle."

"What about my sandwich?" Sam wants to know. "Mom puts plastic wrap on it to keep it nice and fresh."

"Put it in a container with a lid!" Ari says. "That's what my dad does."

"Look! Another worm!" Sam yells. "Right by Mrs. D.!"

I scoop up poor Mrs. Worm, and carry her back to Uncle Ken's Kitchen Composter.

"My dad says the only thing you have to fear is fear itself," John Carmine Tabanelli says.

"I don't get it," Harvey Baxter says.

Mrs. D. sighs. "That means there's really nothing to be afraid of. Come here, Lola. Let me take a closer look at the worm."

I bring the red wiggler up to Mrs. D.

"If you want a closer look, you have to stand still," I tell her.

She stops shuffling around. I hold out Mrs. Worm on my hand. Mrs. D. takes a good look.

"Okay!" she says. "Not afraid, all good."

Then she *clap, clap, clap-clap-claps*. I guess to calm herself down. Finally, Mrs. D. takes a big breath and says, "What do you say, Candy Corns? Should we have two Going Green winners? And two projects?"

"Yay!" the class shouts.

Amanda and I clap high fives. We do our secret Peanut Butter and Jelly handshake and say, "Ooga booga! Ooga! Booga!" 'cause we don't care if Gwendolyn Swanson-Carmichael thinks we're doodle heads.

"Can I learn it, too?" Jessie Chavez asks. "That handshake?"

Our secret handshake? No way! Three's a crowd. That's what I want to say. Also: go away, Jessie!

Jessie is a big problem.

But Mrs. D. tells us to be problem solvers.

"How about a new one for three kids?" I say. "It could be a Bacon, Lettuce, and Tomato secret handshake."

Jessie squishes her nose. "Well, how about a Peanut Butter and Jelly and Banana handshake?"

Amanda puts her hand on my arm. "That sounds—"

"Not so good," I say. I cross my arms right over my heart. "How about a Bacon, Lettuce, and Tomato secret handshake?" I stick my chin way out there, 'cause I'm not fooling around.

"How about Tomato, Lettuce, and Cheese?" she asks.

"You're the Cheese," I say.

"Only if I'm Swiss," she says.

"Fine," I say.

Amanda heaves out a sigh. She wraps one arm around me and another one around that Jessie. And she squeezes us tight together.

"Ooga booga! Ooga! Booga!" we three yell.

Problem solved.

Maybe.

THE KIDS IN MRS. DEBENEDETTI'S SECOND GRADE CLASS (ALPHABETICAL ORDER)

Amanda Anderson

Harvey Baxter

Dilly Chang

Jessie Chavez

Abby Frank

Charlie Henderson

Sam Noonan

Sophie Nunez

Olivia O'Donnell

Madison Rogers

Rita Rohan

Ari Shapiro

Ruby Snow

Jamal Stevenson

Gwendolyn Swanson-Carmichael

John Carmine Tabanelli

Timo Toivonen

Ben Wexler

Lola Zuckerman

SNEAK PREVIEW OF

Last-But-Not-Least

LOLA

AND THE WILD CHICKEN

BOOK TWO

1. A JELLY-BEAN PLAN

MY NAME IS LOLA ZUCKERMAN,

and Zuckerman means I'm always last. Just like
zippers, zoom, and zebras. Last. Zilch, zeroes, and
zombies. Last.

ZZZZZZZ when you're too tired to stay awake.
ZZZZZZZZ when a bee is about to sting you. Z. Ding-
dong LAST in the alphabet.

Every single day, my teacher, Mrs. D., lets us out
in alphabetical order. Every single day, my best
friend Amanda Anderson zips out the door first, and
then Harvey Baxter, Dilly Chang, and Jessie Chavez.
And guess what else? I'll tell you. Every single day
Amanda sits with Jessie on the bus going home.
Even though they live on the same street and
you'd think that would be PLENTY of time to spend
together. But NO. You'd be wrong. Dead wrong.

If only my name was Lola Adventure. Or Lola
Amazing. Or Lola Awesome. Even if I was Lola

Butterbean or Lola Bowling Ball, I'd beat out Chavez every time. But no. I'm stuckerman with Lola Zuckerman.

BRIIIING! The last bell rings. Time to go home.

Mrs. D. says, "Lollipops, time for dismissal," and begins calling our names.

I wait and wait and wait. I hang off my chair. Past the whole alphabet. Finally Mrs. D. says, "Last but not least, Lola, line up."

I skip to the end of the line, lickety-split.

"Lola, stop breathing on my neck," Ben Wexler says.

"Lola, take a step back, please," Mrs. D. says. Fishsticks! I take a step back.

"Gumdrops, don't forget to have your parents sign the field trip permission slip," Mrs. D. tells us. "Our trip to Kookamut Farm is going to be a wonderful experience."

I double-check my permission-slip pocket on my Lola dress. Yep, safe and sound. I pat my marble pocket and peek inside. Except today I don't have my lucky white marble that looks like a dead man's eyeball zipped in there. I've got something else. A secret weapon.

Mrs. D. leads us out the door. As we walk, I fish around in my pocket for a jelly bean. My hand sweated on them a little. But I bet they still taste good. I hold one out to Ben Wexler.

"Can I trade places?" I ask him. He nods and takes the jelly bean. And I get in front of him. I pass a jelly bean to Timo Toivonen and take his place. I work my way up the line, past Gwendolyn Swanson-Carmichael, past Ruby Snow. All the way until I'm behind Jessie Chavez.

"Hey," Jessie says. "You cut."

"Did not. I traded." I hold out a jelly bean. A nice green one. "Wanna trade? I stand in front of you and you get my jelly bean."

Jessie stares at the green jelly bean. Slowly she shakes her head.

"Tell you what," I say. I reach into my pocket and fish out another jelly bean. "I'll make it two." That second jelly bean is a real humdinger. It's a weird one, a double jelly bean. It's pink-pink, with tiny bits of light pink. It's all the pink a pink stinker could want.

Jessie stares at the double jelly bean, plus the green jelly bean. "Fine," she says. "Let's trade." She snatches those jelly beans and pops the green one in her mouth. *Zloop.* She pops the pink one in her pocket.

I squeeze in front of Jessie Chavez and behind Dilly Chang and Harvey Baxter. I can see over them. Straight to Amanda Anderson.

"Hi, Amanda!" I holler-whisper. 'Cause we have to use our inside voices even when we're practically out the door.

Amanda likes The Rules. That's why she doesn't turn around. I bet.

"Amanda! Yoo-hoo!" I yodel-lady-who.

She finally looks at me. Amanda's brown eyes get big and her brown eyebrows pop up. "Lola, what are you doing!?" she says. "You can't cut in line. 'Member?"

"I didn't!" I explain. "I traded my way up."

"Oh!" she says. Then she turns around and—OW OW OW—she smacks right into the closed door instead of following Mrs. D. through the open one.

She stumbles this way and that way, holding her face.

Mrs. D. whips around. "Amanda, are you okay?" Mrs. D. hollers it out loud and I holler it in my brain.

"I'm fine," she squeaks between her fingers in a Not-Fine and It's-Lola's-Fault voice.

"Lola Zuckerman," Mrs. D. barks. "We've already talked about this."

"Okay," I say and slither to the back of the line. Lizards slither and snakes slither and so do kids who have to go all the way to the end of the line. Minus sixteen jelly beans.

Finally, I climb on board bus one. Sure enough, Jessie and Amanda are nestled in tight like two baby kangaroos in one pouch.

"You always get to sit with Amanda on the way home," I tell Jessie. "Can I sit with her today? Pretty please?"

"No way, José. You're not supposed to get up once you sit down."

That's true. That's one of Sal's bus rules. Also, two to a seat. Not three.

Sal starts up the bus and we plant our tushies and glue our eyes straight ahead. Except I hear giggles so I sneak a look around and say, "What's so funny?"

Amanda shrugs and Jessie shrugs.

"Nothing," Jessie mutters like a toothless old man.

"Your forehead is purply," I whisper to Amanda. "Does that hurt?" Poor, poor, poor Amanda.

Amanda touches her forehead and scrunches

up her face. "That's 'cause you distracted me when you cut in line." Uh-oh. She sounds miffed. Miffed is mad but you're not saying.

Maybe it was my fault. My heart aches like it walked into double doors, and the rest of me doesn't feel good, either. Something's tickling me on the tip of my tongue and I think it's "sorry."

"I'm sorry," I say. "I just wanted to sit with you." I dig out a couple of jelly beans. "Here, Amanda. This'll make you feel better."

I plop the jelly beans in her hand. One is purple like her head and one is black. It turns your teeth black when you chew it. Amanda will love that.

She smiles at me with boring white teeth. "Thanks, Lola!"

Jessie shakes her finger. "Jelly beans won't make her head better! You're lucky Amanda didn't get knocked out."

I get up on my knees and lean over my seat. "You're lucky I don't take back that pink jelly bean."

"No take-backs, Lola Zuckerman," Jessie growls like a vicious Chihuahua.

"Lola!" Sal yells. "We talked about this!"

"Okay!" I plant my tushie double fast. He means last week when I got up on my knees and we turned a corner and I fell into the aisle. It was fun except not for Sal.

Sal zooms down the road. I twist around again. Amanda and Jessie are doing the Hand Jive. That's an old-time hand game that Jessie's mom taught her.

"Can I play?" I ask. Sal drives over a pothole and I bounce into the air.

"You can't play," Jessie says, "'cause you weren't there when we learned it."

"Lola, face forward before you get in trouble," Amanda says.

"I can learn," I say. "I learn fast." I stick my hands in the middle of their Hand Jive.

"OW!" Jessie screams. "You POKED ME!"

Our bus whips over to the side of the road. And guess what? It's nobody's stop.

"Lola!" Sal points to me. "Come up here and sit behind me."

I stomp up to the seat where you can count fourteen freckles on Sal's bald head. Where bad kids sit. "Move over, Harvey," I say.

"Can't."

"Why not?"

"I'm glued to the seat. See?" Harvey grunts and pretends he can't move.

The bus starts up and Sal turns the big wheel. "Sit down, Lola," he calls out in a mainly mean but tiny-bit-nice voice. "I don't want to have to tell you again. That goes for you, too, Harvey."

I shove Harvey over and sit down partly on him.

"*Oof!* You crushed me. You weigh more than my dog!"

Harvey is rude like that. He probably missed school on Be-a-Bully-Buster Day.

Sal drives over another pothole and we bounce. Harvey shouts, "Yahoo!" And keeps on bouncing.

Now he's hopping and popping like popcorn in the microwave. "*Hippety, hoppety, hippety, hoppety,*" Harvey sings at the top of his lungs.

"Quiet up there!" Jessie Chavez yells.

"You be quiet, Jessie!" I holler back. "Stop it, Harvey! Stop!" I hiss.

"Can't. Stop," Harvey puffs. "Got to. Break. World record."

"Record for what?"

"Hopping in my bus seat."

Sal pulls up to the stop on Windy Hill Drive. Jessie and Amanda boing up and squeeze down the aisle.

"Bye, Lola," they call out at the same time, just like they practiced it.

"Bye," I say, all by my lonesome self.

Amanda pauses at the top of the stairs. "I'll sit with you on the way to school tomorrow."

I smile big as a slice of watermelon. *Whew!*
I'm glad Amanda isn't mad at me for distracting
her right into the double doors. Amanda waves
goodbye and hops one-two-three off the bus.

And then I think of something.

I get out of my seat and lean over the two teensy
kindergarten kids across the aisle. I bang on their
window. "AMANDA!" I yell. "AMANDA, WILL YOU
SIT WITH ME ON THE FIELD TRIP TO KOOKAMUT
FARM?"

But Amanda and Jessie are skipping down Windy
Hill Drive in front of Amanda's mom.

Amanda can't hear me. Otherwise she would say
yes.

I'll call her soon as I get home. We'll make a plan
to sit together on the field trip. We'll pet chickens.
We'll learn about harvesting fall crops. We'll pick
apples, red for me and yellow for Amanda. We'll get
Friend-of-a-Farmer badges. And Jessie can sit with
Gwendolyn.

It's the perfect plan.